FAIRY NUFF

FAIRY NUFF

a tale of
Bluebell Wood

Herbie Brennan

illustrated by Ross Collins

BLOOMSBURY
CHILDREN'S
BOOKS

Published by Bloomsbury, New York and London
Distributed to the trade by St. Martin's Press

Library of Congress Cataloging-in-Publication Data:
Brennan, Herbie.
Fairy Nuff / Herbie Brennan; Ross Collins, illustrator. –1st U.S. ed. p.cm.
Summary: After mistakenly burning down his own cottage,
Fairy Nuff finds that not only are the Widow Buhiss and some African ants after him,
but also that the Queen urgently needs his help.
ISBN 1-58234-770-0 (alk. paper) ·
[1. Kings, queens, rulers, etc. – Fiction. 2. Ants–Fiction.
3. England–Fiction. 4. Humorous stories.] I. Collins, Ross, ill. II. Title.
PZ7.B75153 Fai 2002
[Fic]–dc21
2001043904

First U.S. Edition
Printed in Great Britain

1 3 5 7 9 10 8 6 4 2

Bloomsbury USA Children's Books
175 Fifth Avenue
New York, New York 10010

For Aynia and Sian,
my darling daughters – H.B.

One

Nuff was far too young to have a first name, so most people called him Fairy Nuff on account of his slim build and pointy ears. He had an elder brother called Biggie, a sister called Sweetie and two parents both named Oldie, which was confusing when you only wanted to talk to one of them. They all lived happily together in a charming little cottage deep in the heart of Bluebell Woo—

Well actually they didn't. Oldie Nuff and Oldie Nuff couldn't stand their children so they went to live with Oldie Nuff's wife's brother Jung E. Nuff in

Switzerland. Sweetie Nuff moved in with an aunt from India named Sari Nuff. Biggie Nuff found a home with a distant cousin on his father's side called Lily Nuff.

This left Fairy Nuff in sole possession of the charming little cottage, but he burned it down trying to light a candle the night everybody left.

This is the way Fairy Nuff tried to light the candle:

First he took the candle from the candleholder and balanced it on top of a barrel full of grey-black powder.

Since he wanted the candlelight to show through the cottage window, he lifted the barrel onto several bales of bone-dry straw and propped it in place with logs and lumps of coal.

He wrapped thirty-two copies of the *Daily Mirror* around the logs and coal. (The headline on one of them said QUEEN KIDNAPPED, but he ignored it because the paper was three days old.)

Next he poured a gallon of gasoline over the candle to make sure the wick would catch. Then he tore the paper label off the barrel (it read *Danger: Gunpowder*) and folded it into a long stick.

He lit the stick with a match and lit the candle with the stick.

When he came to, he was lying in the damp grass with a black face and the cottage was a smoking ruin.

Two

Although Fairy Nuff didn't know it, the cottage hadn't burned down quietly.

There were eighteen wooden packing cases stored in the loft beneath the straw-thatched roof. Eight of them were stencilled with the letters TNT, ten were stencilled with the letters DYNAMITE.

Fortunately all these cases were empty.

Beside them, stored in several tatty suitcases, were Oldie Nuff's souvenirs of World War One. There were five bandoleers of bullets, eighty-two live hand-grenades, seven unexploded German bombs and a large packet of moldy field rations labelled *Hard Tack*.

When Fairy Nuff lit the candle, the gasoline fumes ignited with a *whoosh*, causing the barrel labelled *Danger: Gunpowder* to explode violently, blowing out windows and throwing out Fairy Nuff.

While Fairy Nuff lay outside unconscious on the damp grass, the straw caught fire, igniting the logs and coal which burned fiercely in the cottage living room, lighting the curtains, furniture, wallpaper and the dusty wooden floor.

All these things burned like tinder and the flames rose upwards, as flames do, until they set fire to the roof beams.

These beams – finest oak every one – burned with such vigor that they soon had the floor of the loft ablaze. This naturally caused the wooden packing cases to catch and they, in turn, set fire to the tatty suitcases.

The hard tack inside flared so violently that it caused the bandoleers of bullets to explode in all directions, shooting the safety pins out of eighty-one of the eighty-two live hand grenades. The pin-less hand grenades fragmented instantly to set off the unexploded German bombs.

The bombs, though old, took off the entire roof and hurled it as a flaming ball of fiery thatch beyond Bluebell Wood, beyond the stream that watered Farmer Trench's meadow via Farmer Trench's trench and all the way into the property of Widow Buhiss.

So while Fairy Nuff was still knocked out, his troubles really started.

Three

Widow Buhiss lived alone since her husband died in self-defense. At least she *sort of* lived alone. She shared her enormous, gloomy mansion with countless spiders, rats, bats, toads and frogs. The spiders were extremely hairy. The rats, bats, toads and frogs were mainly bald.

Her mansion was surrounded by over-grown grounds. These were tended by Orc the groundskeeper who lived in the cellar of a ruined gate lodge near the rusting gates. The grounds were full of nightshade, henbane, wolfsbane, aconite, thorn-apple and other poiso-nous plants. The potting shed was packed with insect-eating Venus fly-traps.

Run-down, poisonous and vermin-ridden though it was, the Buhiss Estate stretched for more than 1,200 acres. The wall around it was almost five miles long. If the great flaming fireball hurtling out of Bluebell Wood had landed almost anywhere in this vast wilderness, the chances are that neither Orc nor Widow Buhiss would have noticed.

But it didn't land almost anywhere. It landed on the kennel of Gestapo, Widow Buhiss's pet pit bull terrier.

The kennel was encrusted with toad-stools and other fungi. Its rotting timbers were so damp they actually put out the falling roof. But as Gestapo emerged from the hissing, steaming, smoking heap of burnt-out thatch and charred roof timbers, his eye was caught by what looked like a cooked pineapple lying on the ground nearby. It was the eighty-second hand grenade, the last of Oldie Nuff's surviving World War One souvenirs.

But Gestapo was too young to remember World War One. He pounced on the pineapple and shook it experimentally. Then he tossed it high in the air and watched it crash down on the courtyard cobbles. The pineapple bounced so he caught it in his mouth and shook it violently again. Then he trotted off to show this interesting new toy to his mistress.

As he did so, the ring-pull of the safety pin caught on a thorn bush and jerked out.

At once the hand grenade began to tick.

Four

Widow Buhiss saw the flaming mass of the Nuff cottage roof through her upstairs window and thought it was the end of the world. She waited patiently for earthquake, famine, pestilence and flood. When nothing else happened, she pulled on a stole she'd stolen and teetered downstairs on her best pink high-heeled slippers.

As she reached the hall, Gestapo rattled through the dog-flap in the front door. He was carrying a ticking hand grenade in his mouth. He bounded forward when he saw her, wagging his tail with delight.

"*Eeek!*" shrieked Widow Buhiss who knew a ticking hand grenade when she saw one. "Get away from me at once,

you stupid brute!"

Gestapo dropped the hand grenade and watched it roll across the marble flag-stones until it came to rest beside her feet. He thought she might throw it for him, the way Orc sometimes threw a ball. But Widow Buhiss gathered up her flowing skirts and leaped high in the air. *"Eeek!"* she shrieked again. *"Eeek, eeek! Eeek, eeek!"*

She leaped so high she bounded not just over the ticking hand grenade, but over Gestapo himself. She landed in a brief karate crouch, then aimed a kick at his backside. "Take it out!" she screamed. "Take it out! Take it out!"

Fortunately the kick missed (other-wise Gestapo would have had her leg off) but she was so unbalanced she fell flat on her back. Gestapo trotted to retrieve the hand grenade and carried it across the hall to drop it beside her head. He wagged his tail again and beadied at her with his slinty eyes.

Widow Buhiss swung her legs above her head in a perfect backwards roll, regained her feet, swung around and crashed right through the rotted front door in a splintering of wood and glass.

Still screaming resolutely, she ran across the courtyard and onto the lawn. Puffballs popped beneath her pounding feet.

"Aaargh!" screamed the Widow Buhiss like a retreating steam train. *"Aaargh, aaaaargh, aaaaaaaaargh!"*

Gestapo swooped to grab the hand grenade, then set off after her delightedly.

It was the most fun game he'd ever played.

Five

Orc the groundskeeper was in his new glasshouse while all this was going on.

The glasshouse was enormous and expensive. It was designed to grow rare, exotic South American jungle plants that ate people if they came too close. There were seven of these plants already planted. They stood about the height of a small pony and looked like a vegetarian octopus. They had bright orange, spiny mouths on the top of their massive stems. Their thick, knotted vines and tendrils waved gently, searching for someone to eat.

Orc was spreading horse manure on their roots with a long-handled fork when the distant sound of Widow Buhiss's screams came wafting on the humid air: *"Aaargh, aaaaargh, aaaaaaaaargh!"*

"Hark," frowned Orc, cupping one hand around his good ear.

"Aaargh, aaaaargh, aaaaaaaaargh!"

Orc set down the fork and shuffled from the glasshouse, dragging his club foot. He was a very broad, squat, hairy, muscular man with strangler's hands and one eye lower than the other.

"Aaargh, aaaaargh, aaaaaaaaargh!"

Widow Buhiss was sprinting across

the lawn, her skirts flying wildly. Gestapo was in hot pursuit. She spotted Orc and swerved in his direction. "Save me!" she shouted. "Shoot the dog!"

Orc thought about it for a while, then decided he didn't have a gun. So he placed two horse-manure-encrusted fingers into his mouth and whistled. The sound shattered a pane in his glasshouse and attracted Gestapo's attention. The dog stopped chasing Widow Buhiss and turned to bound towards Orc instead. He had a ball in his mouth.

"Decapitate him! Crush him! Smash him! Beat him to a pulp! He's got a bomb!" ordered Widow Buhiss breathlessly as she headed for the far horizon.

Gestapo dropped his ball at Orc's feet, then bounced back expectantly. Orc blinked. Now that the Widow mentioned it, the ball did look very like a hand grenade. He picked it up and listened to the tick.

Orc's brain lurched forward a small notch. He drew back his arm and hurled the hand grenade with all the strength at his command.

Gestapo waited patiently for somebody to say, *"Fetch!"*

Six

Since Orc was very strong, the hand grenade described a great, high arc and sailed, as if in slow motion, right over the tall wall that surrounded the Buhiss estate.

Beyond the tall wall was a lonely trunk road (the N87 to be exact). On the lonely trunk road, rattling, squealing and backfiring, was an original Model T Ford, lovingly, but not well, restored by its driver, a solicitor named Silas Snodgrass.

Solicitor Snodgrass had driven slowly all the way from London to bring good news to Widow Buhiss. An ancient aunt who lived in Perth, Australia, had died and left her shares in several gold mines worth twenty thousand billion pounds. The share certificates were made out to 'Bearer' and locked up in a leather brief-case on the back seat of the car.

As Snodgrass approached the entrance to the estate, the rusty gates flung open and Widow Buhiss sped out. Snodgrass recognized her at once from a photograph in his possession. He applied the hand brake, honked the horn and waited for his Model T to lumber to a halt.

"Widow Buhiss!" he exclaimed. "How fortunate to meet you in this way!"

"Bog off!" snapped Widow Buhiss. She began to leg it down the road.

"But I have your legacy with me, Widow Buhiss," Solicitor Snodgrass

called after her. "It's shares worth twenty thousand billion pounds."

Widow Buhiss stopped abruptly. "Did you say shares?" she whispered. "Did you say twenty thousand billion pounds?"

She turned in time to see Gestapo's hand grenade arc across the wall and fall towards the car. Since Model Ts do not possess a roof, it dropped into the back seat where it landed on the briefcase, ticking loudly.

Solicitor Snodgrass removed his spectacles, polished them briefly with his hanky, then put them on again to peer closely at the bomb. "Good grief!" he said before jumping from his car and racing down the middle of the road.

"Nooooo!" wailed Widow Buhiss, who knew full well what was about to happen.

The ticking stopped.

The hand grenade exploded.
Share certificates were strewn in all directions. A sudden wind sprang up and carried them away.

Seven

"My share certificates!" screamed Widow Buhiss.

"My Model T!" wailed Solicitor Snodgrass.

Solicitor Snodgrass stalked off towards London determined to sue someone. Widow Buhiss stalked through the rusty gates into her poisonous estate determined to kill someone. Orc the groundskeeper was heading back toward his glasshouse when she caught up with him.

"Who sent us a bomb?" she demanded.

"Search me," said Orc.

"Where did Gestapo find it?" she demanded.

"Search me," said Orc.

Widow Buhiss looked furiously around and saw the burnt-out remains of the Nuff cottage roof piled up on Gestapo's kennel. "Who tried to set fire to Gestapo?" she demanded.

"Search me," said Orc.

It was all too much. Widow Buhiss threw a wobbler. Her body began to shake, her toes to curl. Her nostrils flared, her eyes blazed. Her face flushed when she pulled her ear. Her hands

curled into fists. Beads of sweat broke on her forehead. Her hair turned red and stood on end. Steam poured from her nose. Her foot tapped uncontrollably. Her knees cracked like pistol shots. Her elbows turned bright green. Her head glowed. Her mouth writhed. Her lips pouted. Her legs jerked. Her right hand gripped her throat and tried to strangle her. Her left hand fought it off.

"Who made me lose twenty thousand

billion pounds worth of share certificates?" she howled.

"Search me," said Orc, who'd seen it all before.

Widow Buhiss's cheek began to twitch. "I will find him," she hissed furiously. "I will search him out. I will search in the valleys and the hills. I will search in the houses and the sheds. I will seek him in the fields and the meadows. I will look by the sea-shore. I will harrow the deep woods. I will examine the mountains and the rivers. I will find him if it takes me to the ends of the earth or the depths of the ocean. Nobody, but nobody, costs Jennett Buhiss twenty thousand billion pounds and gets away with it!"

"Fair enough," said Orc.

"Fairy Nuff?" screamed Widow Buhiss. "You mean that skinny boy with pointy ears who lives in Bluebell Wood? You tell me it was Fairy Nuff? Fairy Nuff burned out my dog? Fairy Nuff sent us a hand grenade? Fairy Nuff lost my money?" She took such a deep breath that her eyes crossed and her chest swelled like a pigeon's. There was a moments deep and profound silence.

Then ....

Then ....

Then ....

Then Widow Buhiss turned her face
towards the heavens and released a
mighty roar:

"BRING ME THE HEAD OF FAIRY
NUFF!"

Eight

The first thing Fairy Nuff saw when he came to was the smoking ruin of his family cottage. *Ooops!* he thought.

The next thing he saw was a very broad, squat, hairy, muscular figure with strangler's hands and one eye lower than the other, dragging its club foot towards him. *Yipes!* he thought.

He jumped to his feet and looked

around. The cottage was set in a clearing deep inside Bluebell Wood. If it had still been standing, he might have run inside and locked the door. If the woodshed had still been standing, he could have grabbed an axe to drive the dreadful man away. If the garden shed had still been standing, he could have hit him with a spade or poked him with a fork. If –

But nothing was still standing. The sheds and the axe and the fork and the spade had all been reduced to ash and slag by the fierce heat of the fire. There was nothing left that Fairy Nuff could use to defend himself, nowhere he could run to hide.

Except, of course, for Bluebell Wood itself, which had stubbornly refused to burn down.

Fairy Nuff had taken three strides towards the trees when a thought struck him.

The thought was, *Why am I running?*

The figure shuffling towards him was certainly ugly. It certainly had strangler's hands. It certainly had a strange gleam in its uneven eyes. But what of that, thought Fairy Nuff? Might not this creature have a kind heart? Might it not have a sunny disposition? Might it not have a gentle nature? Was it not possible for someone to be both ugly and good? Could a man not be hideous and kind? Should one judge only by appearances? Was it not beholden on Fairy Nuff to give this poor unfortunate the benefit of the doubt?

Fairy Nuff stopped. He turned. He smiled his sweetest smile. "Good sir, tell me your name," he said softly.

"Orc," Orc sniffed, for it was he.

"Pray, good sir," asked Fairy Nuff, "why are you shuffling towards me?"

"I've come for the head of Fairy Nuff," said Orc, flexing his strangler's fingers.

Fairy Nuff bolted for the trees.

Nine

The most dangerous thing in Bluebell
Wood (except for Fairy Nuff when he
was lighting candles) was an ant colony
that had emigrated from Africa to
escape religious persecution.

The ants in this colony were larger
than standard English ants and even
somewhat larger than the muscular
Scottish highland ants who fought the
spider threatening Robert the Bruce.
They had enormous mandibles, which is
what ants call jaws, and antennae long
enough to pick up signals from alien
ants in Outer Space.

In Africa, these ants lived on a diet of
elephants. Since there were no elephants

in Bluebell Wood, they now ate snow-drops, bluebells, daisies, honeysuckle and various root vegetables, depending on the season. But they still longed for elephant meat and were hungry almost all the time.

The colony was ruled by a royal family consisting of the Queen Ant, the Queen Ant's mother, known as the Queen Mother Ant, and the Queen Ant's aunt, known as the Queen Aunt Ant.

The duties of the Queen Mother Ant

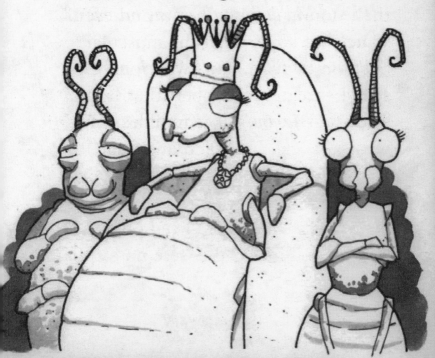

and the Queen Aunt Ant were quite light – they waved from their respective balconies twice a day – but life was very different for the Queen Ant. Although she had grown so fat she seldom left her Throne Room, nothing could be done in the colony unless the Queen Ant said so.

There was a constant stream of ordinary ants through the Throne Room, all asking permission of the Queen Ant for one thing or another:

Please, Ma'am, may I eat my breakfast?
Yes!
Please, Ma'am, may I scratch my ear?
Yes!
Please, Ma'am, may I wave back to

the Queen Mother Ant?

Yes!

And so on, day and night.

Because the weather in Bluebell Wood was less sunny than Africa and there were no elephants to eat, the ants in the colony were very bad-tempered. The Queen Ant, who got very little sleep, was the most bad-tempered of them all.

This bad-tempered colony had built an anthill, the like of which never seen before in Bluebell Wood. It was conical in shape, made from tightly-packed earth, and fully six feet tall.

When Fairy Nuff bolted into Bluebell Wood, he ran straight into it.

Ten

"Ooof!" exclaimed Fairy Nuff.

"Head," grunted Orc the groundskeeper, who was not all that far behind him.

Although winded, Fairy Nuff still knew what would happen to him if Orc managed to catch up. He ran around the massive anthill and blundered off the path into the bushes.

Loping along behind him, Orc grinned evilly to himself. In the years he'd worked for Widow Buhiss, he'd got used to hacking through the undergrowth. That meant he would soon catch up with Fairy Nuff.

His large, purple tongue lolled out to lick his large purple lips. "Head," he

murmured. "Bring the Widow back his head, head, head, head, head."

Fairy Nuff crashed and clattered through the bushes for a while, his face and hands scratched by briars, his trousers ripped by thorns. When his cottage exploded his boots had blown off so now his feet were being bruised by stones. He felt utterly miserable, but he still wanted to hold onto his head.

"Head ..." echoed Orc somewhere behind him.

Orc was finding life much easier. With his special skills finely honed in the poison wilderness of the Buhiss Estate, he was able to slip through the under-growth with the grace and skill of a prima ballerina. He would pirouette to one side as the briars reached for him, perform a twinkling pas de deux in order to escape the thorns. He looked extremely silly, but he suffered far less damage than the boy ahead.

The boy ahead, Fairy Nuff, broke free at last from thorns and brambles to find himself beside an open river. On his right was a wooden bridge that went from the near bank to the far bank. On his left was a metal bridge that went from the far bank to the near bank.

Fairy Nuff hesitated, confused about which bridge to take. Obviously he could not take the metal bridge that led from the far bank to the near bank since

he was not yet on the far bank.

But if he took the wooden bridge from the near bank to the far bank, he might never be able to get back again since, having reached the far bank, he would no longer be on the near bank.

He was still struggling with the problem when Orc made a graceful leap out of the thicket to land on top of him.

"Gotcha!" Orc said, reaching for his head.

Eleven

When Fairy Nuff ran into the anthill, the vibrations of the impact carried through the breeding gallery and the feeding gallery, the building store and the gilding store, the water chamber and the hotter chamber, all the way to the Throne Room.

An ant who had been about to ask permission to go to the loo, asked instead, "What was that?"

"Something has blundered into our

collective home," the Queen Ant told it.

"Kill! Kill! Kill!" chanted several soldier ants.

"Yes, presently, my dears," the Queen Ant shushed them.

A messenger ant hurled itself breathlessly into the Throne Room.

"Something has blundered into our collective home!" it reported.

"We know that!" snapped the Queen Ant. "Go and find out what it was!"

"And kill it," muttered the worst-tempered soldier ant.

As the messenger ant raced out again,

all the other ants stood still and listened. Almost at once they heard the sound of something crashing through the undergrowth.

The ant who wanted to go to the loo hesitated, then curiosity got the better of it. "What was that?" it asked again. There was a long, quiet silence in the Throne Room. Every ant was looking at the Queen. The Queen glanced to her right and thought. She glanced to her left and thought some more. She looked up to the ceiling and pondered. She looked down to the floor and considered.

"I think it must have been an elephant," she said at last.

"An elephant?" blinked the ant who wanted to go to the loo.

"An elephant?" echoed the ant behind it.

"Food?" asked a soldier ant.

"Hunt down the elephant!" the Queen commanded.

Every ant in the entire throne room turned and raced towards the door. Scent messages were wafted on the air. Soldiers fell in, hunters turned out, elephant traps were dusted off, elephant nets were carefully untangled, elephant lures were taken from their storage boxes. In moments the entire ant colony was on the move.

"Go! Go! Go!" the Queen demanded.

At once the ants began to swarm towards the main gates of the anthill. The messenger ant, returning with the news that all the fuss was being made by one thin boy, was trampled under foot. A black torrent of hungry ants poured into Bluebell Wood. Some were as big as roaches, some as beetles, some as mice.

All of them headed after Fairy Nuff.

Twelve

"What's this?" sniffed Widow Buhiss when Orc the groundskeeper dragged the struggling boy into her living room.

"It's Fairy Nuff," Orc muttered.

"It may seem fair enough to you," snapped Widow Buhiss, "but I told you to bring back his head."

"It was attached to his body," Orc said, "so I brung them both."

"Well detach it now!" cried Widow Buhiss. "And give the rest of him to your man-eating plants."

"They only eat live food and Chinese take-out," Orc said. "They're very picky."

Widow Buhiss gave a long-suffering

sigh. "Oh, very well," she said. "Lock
him in the woodshed with the other one
and we'll feed them to the plants after
supper. There's nothing good on televi-
sion anyway."

Orc tucked Fairy Nuff beneath one
massive arm and carried him out of the

house towards the woodshed. Since he was being carried head down, Fairy Nuff couldn't see where he was going, but he heard Orc unlocking several locks and chains before he was turned right way up and pushed inside.

"Stay there!" growled Orc and slammed the door.

Fairy Nuff picked himself up off the floor of the woodshed. He rushed to the door Orc just slammed shut. "Let me out!" he shouted. "Let me out at once!" He pounded on the wooden panels, making a great deal of noise. But not quite enough to drown the sound of Orc locking up the locks and chains again.

Fairy Nuff stopped pounding and listened with despair to Orc's receding footsteps. "Let me out!" he whispered. "You can't keep me here. You can't feed me to your plants...." But he whispered only weakly because he knew full well people like Orc and Widow Buhiss could do just about anything they wanted to people like Fairy Nuff and no one would ever know.

Fairy Nuff sniffed. If there had been anyone in the woodshed with him, they might have thought he was actually crying. And they would probably have been right.

After a while, Fairy Nuff stopped feeling sorry for himself and looked around the shed.

That's when he discovered there *was* someone in it with him.

Thirteen

The woman in the woodshed was dressed in ermine-trimmed robes and wearing a diamond-studded crown. She had an orb in one hand and a sceptre in the other. There were glass slippers on her feet.

"Who are you?" asked Fairy Nuff.

"We are the Queen of England," said the woman mournfully.

"You may be, but I'm not," said Fairy Nuff. "And to be honest, I don't think you are either – you're not a bit like your picture on the pennies."

"That's quite an old picture," the woman told him, "and it never did me justice."

"But if you're the Queen of England,"

Fairy Nuff protested, "why aren't you in London in your palace?"

"We were kidnapped four days ago," the woman said. "The *Daily Mirror* was full of it." She frowned. "Although I believe the *Telegraph* only gave me an inside page."

A flash bulb went off in Fairy Nuff's head. He suddenly remembered the headline in the *Daily Mirror* he had used to wrap the logs and coal he'd used to prop up the gunpowder barrel supporting the candle he was lighting when his home blew up.

The headline said, QUEEN KIDNAPPED.

He peered at the woman closely. On second thought she really did look a little like the picture on the pennies. And it occurred to him very few women dressed in ermine and carried orbs and sceptres. But what was the Queen of England

doing in Widow Buhiss' woodshed?

Fairy Nuff decided to sort that out later and fell on one knee. "Your Majesty, I am your loyal subject, Fairy Nuff."

"That's fair enough by me," the Queen said. "But how are you going to get us out of here?"

Fairy Nuff looked around. Since he was still down on one knee, he had to twist and turn a lot. But twist and turn as he might, it was difficult to see a way out.

The door was sturdy and secured by several locks. There were two windows, but both were fitted with enormous metal bars. He thought of smashing through the roof, but it was far too high to reach. He wondered about tunnelling underneath the walls, but the floor was made from pre-stressed concrete.

He stopped swivelling around and looked back at the Queen.

"Getting out may be a little difficult," he said.

Fourteen

Widow Buhiss dined alone that evening, a simple meal of sheep's eyes, pickled pig's feet, mad cow brains and goat, washed down by Chateau Margaux, '98.

While waiting for her coffee to perk, she called her favourite nephew in Tasmania.

"That you, Aunt Jennett?" asked the nephew, recognising the grating Buhiss voice. "How's your old didgeri doing?"

"Fine, thank you, Alabaster," Widow

Buhiss said. "I trust I haven't interrupt-ed anything important?"

"Strewth, no, Aunt Jennett – just chasing a few boomers by the billabong. Came back to have a tube of Fosters and a pail of prawns. Everything okay your end?"

Widow Buhiss tossed some goat bones to Gestapo. "More than just okay," she said. "Everything is hunky dory, tickety-boo and wizard prang."

"What about your plan to take over England?" asked Alabaster curiously.

Widow Buhiss gave a little smile. "Well, my dear, that's what I called to tell you. I've managed to kidnap the Queen and lock her in my woodshed."

"Bonzer!" Alabaster exclaimed approv-ingly.

"When I've had my coffee I shall feed her to Orc's man-eating plants. They'll digest everything, you know —"

"Including her glass eye and wig?" Alabaster put in.

"Bones and all!" said Widow Buhiss. "When that's done I shall take her place. We're much alike, you know. Once I put on her ermine robes and crown, no-one will be able to tell the difference."

"So what happens after that?" asked Alabaster curiously.

"Well, the first thing I shall do is fire that ghastly little upstart of a Prime Minister and put Orc in his place. The rest should be plain sailing. I shall make you Governor General of Australia, of course."

"Gee, thanks, Aunt Jennett — that's real dinkum of you. So, no worries then?"

Widow Buhiss waved an airy hand. "Oh, I lost a little money. And there was a silly boy from Bluebell Wood who sent me a hand-grenade." She smiled a sinister smile. "But he's been taken care of now."

"Attagirl, Aunt Jennett!" Alabaster exclaimed enthusiastically.

"Must go now," Widow Buhiss told him. "My coffee's finished perking and I have a great deal still to do."

Fifteen

Orc dined with the man-eating plants, a simple meal of moldy bread and stinky cheese. But he'd bought a Chinese take-out as an appetizer for the plants.

"Just a little snack," he said, tossing barbecued spare ribs and chicken wings towards them. "Just a small morsel to give you an appetite," he grinned, hurling lumps of beef in oyster sauce, pork dumplings, egg-fried rice, dim sum packets, prawn crackers, Peking duck, hundred-year-old eggs, sweet and sour midgets, thick corn soup, lemon mushrooms and the foil trays they came in.

The man-eating plants caught every missile expertly and popped it in their orange

mouths. Those that swallowed trays burped loudly and ejected them. Fronds and tendrils lashed and writhed delightedly.

"Soon get you a proper meal," said Orc, still grinning. "A fairy cake for starter and Queen of Puddings for dessert!" He stuffed bread and cheese into his mouth and laughed at his own wit. Bits of bread and cheese flew out again. "Soon, my beauties, soon," he said.

Widow Buhiss danced into the greenhouse. "Are the plants prepared and ready, Orc?" she trilled.

"Ready as they'll ever be," said Orc.

"Then let's away without delay, that's what I say!" cried Widow Buhiss, scarcely able to contain her excitement.

"Haven't finished my supper yet," Orc muttered.

"But I have finished mine," Widow Buhiss exclaimed grandly, "and that is all that matters. Shake a leg, man, shake a leg!"

Orc crammed the rest of the moldy

bread and stinky cheese into his mouth and hauled himself reluctantly onto his feet. Widow Buhiss linked her arm in his as they walked together from the glasshouse. "I've quite recovered from the loss of my twenty thousand billion pounds," she told him. "Shall I tell you why?"

"Yus," said Orc, "you shall."

"I've quite recovered because when I become Queen I shall tell the Royal Mint to print me *forty* thousand billion pounds. They'll have to do it too, because I shall be the Queen."

"Yus," said Orc, "you shall."

"I can hardly wait," said Widow Buhiss. "Do you think your plants will eat her quickly?"

"Yus," said Orc, "they will."

They walked together to the wood-shed to fetch the Queen and Fairy Nuff.

But when Orc unlocked the door, the Queen and Fairy Nuff were not inside.

Sixteen

"Are you sure?" asked Widow Buhiss, trying to peer over Orc's broad shoulder.

"See for yourself," said Orc.

They both stared into the gloomy woodshed. The window bars were still intact. Nobody had smashed through the roof or tunnelled underneath the walls. Orc himself had seen the door was locked and chained. Yet the only thing now in the woodshed was the stack of logs in the far corner.

"How did they get out?" demanded Widow Buhiss.

"Dunno," said Orc.

"Where did they go to?" screamed Widow Buhiss.

"Dunno," said Orc.

They stepped back and stared about them, hoping to catch sight of the Queen and Fairy Nuff. They stared towards the house, but there was no sign. They stared across the courtyard, but there was no sign. They stared across the lawn, but there was no sign.

They stared towards the main gates, but there was no —

"What's that?" Orc frowned.

"What's what?" frowned Widow Buhiss.

"That by the gates," said Orc.

They stood side by side, Orc and Widow Buhiss, shading their eyes against the setting sun and staring at the black tide pouring through the main gates and along the driveway.

"Eclipse of the sun?" Orc suggested. He thought the black tide might be a shadow.

"Don't be stupid!" snapped the Widow Buhiss. She strained her eyes and squinted as the black tide drew nearer. "It's not the Queen," she said.

"Don't think so," Orc said.

"And it's definitely not that horribly ugly skinny boy."

"Definitely not him," Orc echoed. "Not even slightly like him."

They watched the black tide as it flowed towards them. Faintly at first, but growing louder, Widow Buhiss' ears caught a strange clicking sound. It was as if a great many tiny marching creatures were snapping their mandibles together at the same time.

The Widow Buhiss blinked. "Ants!" she screamed.

"Ants?" asked Orc.

"Huge, fierce, vicious, dangerous ants like the sort they have in Africa!" gasped Widow Buhiss. "Do something! Do something at once!"

Orc did something at once. He ran.

After a moment, Widow Buhiss followed.

Seventeen

The ant at the front of the ant horde that swarmed out of the ant-hill to follow Fairy Nuff (thinking him to be an elephant) was a short-sighted ant called Ant No. 287655439.

The only reason she was at the front was that she happened to be nearest the main gateway when the Queen Ant ordered everybody out to hunt the elephant. But her new position went straight to her head and she began giving orders.

"This way!" ordered Ant No. 287655439. "Keep in line. No dawdling. March faster. No straggling. Eyes front. Keep time. Click mandibles. Follow me."

The other ants, well used to orders, went that way, kept in line, didn't dawdle, marched faster, failed to straggle, held their eyes to the front, kept time, clicked their mandibles and followed her. As a result they soon got lost.

"Keep in step!" ordered Ant No. 287655439 to cover her confusion.

In perfect step the ants followed Ant No. 287655439 into the undergrowth and out again, around the great oak tree and back again, up the little hill and down again, far away and near again until they found themselves in sight of their ant-hill again.

"The Queen Ant's going to kill you," whispered Ant No. 833456321 who was at Ant No. 287655439's shoulder.

"About turn!" ordered Ant No. 287655439.

The ants turned about and headed back into the undergrowth. This time

they managed to march straight enough
to reach the river with the wooden
bridge that went from the near bank to
the far bank and the metal bridge that
went from the far bank to the near bank.

"Break step!" commanded Ant No.
287655439 who'd read somewhere that
if you marched across a bridge in step
the bridge might shake to pieces.

The ants broke step and followed Ant

No. 287655439 across the wooden bridge. Some walked, some limped, some tap-danced, some turned cartwheels, some nose-bounced, some wriggled, some crawled, some bonged on tiny pogo-sticks, but positively not one of them even for a moment marched in step.

Ant No. 287655439 led them all the way across the wooden bridge, down the river bank and all the way across the

metal bridge. Then she led them through the undergrowth and back until they came in sight of their ant-hill again.

"I'll take over," growled Ant No. 833456321, moving to the front.

This is the reason why the ants took so long to reach the front gates of the Buhiss Estate.

Eighteen

"Have they gone?" the Queen whispered.

"I think so," Fairy Nuff whispered back.

"That was a very clever plan," the Queen said, "a very clever plan indeed."

They were crouched together underneath the pile of logs in the corner of the woodshed. Fairy Nuff could see that Orc and Widow Buhiss had left the door wide open. He began to remove the logs, first from the Queen, then from himself.

The Queen brushed wood-chips, moss and sawdust from her ermine and adjusted her diamond crown. "I think I might consider making you a knight, Fairy Nuff."

"Sounds fair enough to me," said Fairy Nuff delightedly.

"But first," the Queen said, "we'd better leg it before those two come back. If they realize we're still here, they'll close the door again."

"I couldn't agree with you more, Your Majesty," said Fairy Nuff.

They moved together to the door of the woodshed and Fairy Nuff peered carefully out. There was no sign of Orc or Widow Buhiss. "I think the coast is clear," he said.

"Then I shall lead the way," said the Queen, who was used to leading the way.

They stepped from the woodshed.

The Queen stopped so suddenly that

Fairy Nuff walked into her bottom. He jumped back hurriedly, wondering if he could be jailed for treason. "I'm terribly sorry, Your Majesty," he said.

"Think nothing of it," the Queen said. "Our consort does it all the time. But why has the Widow Buhiss surrounded us with tar?"

Fairy Nuff looked around the Queen. There was a black moving tide just yards away, but it wasn't tar.

"I think it's ants, Your Majesty," he said.

The Queen put on her glasses. "They seem very large for ants."

They did indeed. They were the largest ants Fairy Nuff had ever seen. The moving carpet crept steadily nearer. "Back to the woodshed, Your Majesty!" he yelled. "The door fits tight enough to keep them out!"

"I think perhaps we shall," the Queen said.

They turned to find the ants were now between them and the woodshed.

"Across the lawn, Your Majesty! We may be able to out-run them!"

"I think perhaps we may," the Queen said.

They turned to find the ants were spread across the lawn.

"The house, Your Majesty," urged Fairy Nuff. "We'll just have to escape them in the house." He hoped Orc and the Widow Buhiss weren't waiting in the house.

"Orc and the Widow Buhiss may be waiting in the house," the Queen protested.

"We have to take that chance!" Fairy Nuff exclaimed.

They turned to find the ants were now between them in the house. They turned and turned and turned and turned, but everywhere they turned the ants approached them.

They were surrounded.

Nineteen

Widow Buhiss found Orc in the glasshouse. He was curled up in a corner with his thumb plugged into his mouth. One of the man-eating plants had a frond around his shoulder and was stroking his bald head reassuringly.

"What's the matter with you?" Widow Buhiss demanded.

"Ants," said Orc. "I hate them!"

"Nonsense!" Widow Buhiss snapped. "Ants have to be tackled like any other problem, with determination and resolve. Now brace up, man, and tackle them!"

But Orc didn't move. "You know ants ate my Uncle Alfred's leg off," he said sullenly.

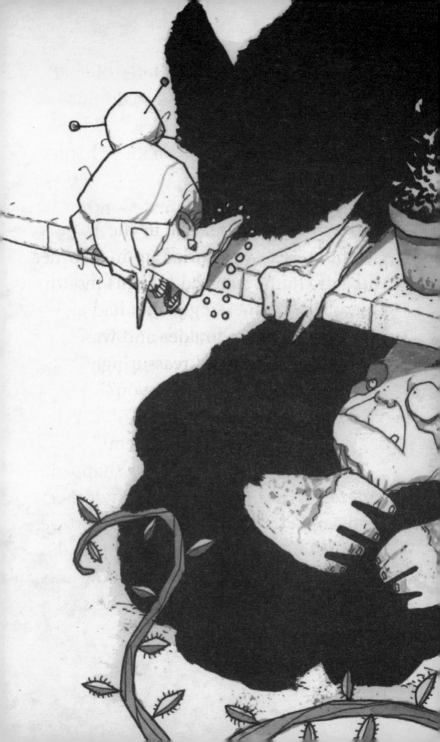

"That was termites – different insect altogether," Widow Buhiss told him. "Besides, it was a wooden leg."

"Don't care," Orc said sulkily. "I still hate ants."

"That may be," exclaimed Widow Buhiss, "but that attitude won't do us any good. If you don't do something about them, they will overrun the entire estate." She sniffed. "Besides, we can't find the Queen and that dreadful boy with ants running all over the place. You must get rid of them at once!"

"Shan't!" said Orc.

The Widow Buhiss wondered briefly if she should throw another wobbler, but decided she didn't really have the time. Instead she walked over briskly, took Orc by the hand and pulled him to his feet. A man-eating plant tendril reached for her, but she slapped it away sharply.

"Pull yourself together, man!" she told Orc sharply. "We're going to the potting shed!"

She turned and dragged him from the glasshouse. Orc began to shake the moment they got outside, but there were no ants nearby. In a moment they were headed for the potting shed.

The potting shed was full of pots. There were pots of paint, pots of jam, pots of pickle, pots of noodle and even pots of other pots. "How can you find anything in here?" demanded Widow Buhiss. "It's enough to drive you potty!"

She walked to a far shelf and took down a pot of powder. "Kills flies, fleas, bugs, wasps, beetles," she read from the label, "lice, mice, silverfish, bookworms, hookworms, tapeworms, silkworms, stray cats, small rats and ... ah yes, just as I thought ... ANTS!!!"

She swung around, brandishing the pot. "This will do the trick, Orc! We'll sprinkle it about. Soon there won't be a single ant on the entire estate!"

But when she went in search of ants, she found the ants already gone.

Twenty

Although Ant No. 833456321 had a better sense of direction than Ant No. 287655439, she was no less short-sighted. So when the ants surrounded Fairy Nuff and the Queen of England, all Ant No. 833456321 could really see was two large, fuzzy shapes.

"Capture the elephants!" she ordered.

At once the hunter ants raced forward to fling their elephant nets over the Queen and Fairy Nuff.

At once the soldier ants raced forward to tie elephant ropes around their legs.

At once the cowboy ants lassoed them around their shoulders.

At once the most muscular ants began

to tug the ropes to topple them onto the
ground.

"Aren't they a bit small for elephants?" asked Ant No. 287655439
now she'd a chance to get a closer look.

"They're English elephants," said Ant
No. 833456321. "English elephants are
very small."

"But aren't they an odd shape for elephants?" asked Ant No. 287655439, who was starting to wonder if she should take back the leadership.

"English elephants are known to look extremely strange," said Ant No. 833456321 decisively. She frowned at Ant No. 287655439. "You aren't thinking of taking back the leadership, are you?"

"No," said Ant No. 287655439 quickly.

Working as a close-knit team, the ants wrapped so many ropes around the Queen and Fairy Nuff that they looked like Egyptian mummies.

"This has been a most successful hunt," Ant No. 833456321 announced.

"Let us now lift these elephants and carry them back home to our hill in Bluebell Wood!"

The ants swarmed underneath the Queen and Fairy Nuff and began to sing their lifting song. The words were rather boring – 'Lift … Lift … Lift' – but it was a catchy tune.

They hoisted Fairy Nuff to shoulder height. "This is quite a light elephant," they said.

They hoisted the Queen to shoulder height. "This is a slightly heavier elephant," they said.

Still singing lustily, they carried the Queen and Fairy Nuff back to the anthill in Bluebell Wood.

Twenty-One

With almost all her colony gone off to hunt elephants, the Queen Ant found herself at a loss for things to do.

Nobody came into the Throne Room to ask if they could eat their breakfast. Nobody wanted permission to scratch their ear. Nobody wished her to rule on whether they might wave back to the Queen Mother Ant.

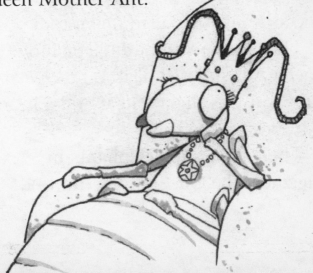

After several hours of this, she grew so bored she left the Throne Room and waved back at the Queen Mother Ant herself. Then she went to the other balcony and waved back to the Queen Aunt Ant.

"Where's everybody gone?" the Queen Aunt Ant called down to her.

"They've gone to hunt elephants," the Queen Ant shouted back. The Queen Aunt Ant was slightly deaf and a bit out of it most of the time.

"There aren't any elephants in England," the Queen Aunt Ant said.

The Queen Ant blinked. "Pardon?"

"I said there aren't any elephants in England," the Queen Aunt Ant repeated. "Unless you count zoos, safari parks and the odd travelling circus. Certainly no elephants in Bluebell Wood. Not

enough for them to eat. We can hardly get by ourselves."

The Queen Ant went back to her Throne Room to have a little think.

She was still thinking when a messenger ant hurtled into the Throne Room. "The Hunt has returned!" it announced.

Two teams of herald ants paraded quickly into the throne room, dressed in gorgeous golds and reds. "Ta-rah!" they sang in unison. "Ta, ta-rah-ra, ta-rah-ra, ta-rah-rah!"

The chief herald stepped forward.

"The Hunt approacheth!" he announced grandly.

He returned to his place. "Ta-rah-rah-rah-rah ... rah-rah!" sang the herald ants in unison.

There was a moment's silence, then the galleries of the ant-hill began to vibrate with the approach of marching feet. *Chump, chump, chump, chump!* they sounded. *Chump, chump, chump, chump!* Nearer and nearer they came, louder and louder the sound.

"Ta-rah. Ta-rah-rah-rah!" sang the herald ants.

"The Hunt is here!" the chief herald roared.

Into the Throne Room marched Ant No. 833456321. "Your Majesty," she called, "we've caught two elephants!"

"Don't be stupid," said the Queen Ant. "There are no elephants in England."

Twenty-Two

"I'd invite you back to my house for a cup of tea," Fairy Nuff told the Queen of England after the ants released them. "But I'm afraid I burned it down."

"Perhaps I could just see where it used to be," the Queen said. "That would be very nice before I have to go back home to London."

As they walked together through Bluebell Wood towards the clearing where the Nuff cottage used to be, Fairy Nuff asked curiously, "What are you going to do about Orc and the Widow Buhiss, Your Majesty?"

The Queen waved one hand airily. "I shall send my Beefeaters to arrest them.

I expect a few years in the Tower will cool them down."

"Quite right," said Fairy Nuff approvingly.

They emerged into the clearing. The ruin of Nuff Cottage had stopped smoking, but otherwise was much as Fairy Nuff remembered it.

"What a charming setting," said the Queen politely.

"Bit of a mess," said Fairy Nuff. It looked as though some litter louts had held a picnic, for there were papers scattered everywhere.

"No matter," said the Queen cheerful-
ly. "It's perfect for what we have to do."
She caught his puzzled look and added,
"We promised we would knight you."

Fairy Nuff blinked. "You mean you
can do it here?"

"Of course I can. Please kneel down –
just there where the ground is dry."

Fairy Nuff went down on one knee.

"Now please avert your eyes while I
get my sword."

Fairy Nuff averted his eyes. The
Queen quickly raised her skirts and
drew a long ceremonial sword from her

knickers. She smoothed her skirts back down again. "You can look now."

"What do you want me to do?" asked Fairy Nuff.

"Just try to keep still," the Queen said. She stepped forward and placed the sword on his right shoulder. It felt quite warm. "We dub thee knight of the realm," she said. She raised the sword and touched it to his left shoulder. "Arise Sir Fairy Nuff!" she said.

His knees cracked loudly as he stood. "Thank you, Your Majesty! I'm very grateful."

"It's the very least I could do for the boy who rescued me," the Queen said firmly. "But now I must be getting back to London."

Sir Fairy Nuff watched proudly as the Queen strode down the path that took her out of Bluebell Wood.

"Goodbye, Your Majesty," he said.

Epilogue

Fairy Nuff stood quite still for a long time after the Queen of England disappeared. Eventually he sighed and turned away. "Better get this place tidied up," he said aloud.

He picked up a piece of paper. It was a share certificate for an Australian goldmine. Printed neatly on the front were the words:

£1 billion.

He picked up another. It too was a share certificate printed with the words £1 billion.

Fairy Nuff looked around. He reckoned there must be twenty thousand bits of paper scattered through the clearing.

Quite suddenly he thought he'd build himself a castle.